MÖLANG

Spooky Halloween

by Lauren Bisom

SCHOLASTIC INC.

10 9 8 7 6 5 4 3 2 1   18 19 20 21 22

ISBN 978-1-338-25958-2

Printed in the U.S.A.   40

First printing 2018
Book design by Becky James and Angela Jun

It's Halloween and Piu Piu is hard at work decorating their yard for the holiday. Piu Piu is even building something extra special.

Molang is curious. What could it be?
It's a scarecrow! Now all that's missing is a big, round pumpkin head.

As Piu Piu gets ready to carve the perfect pumpkin, an elephant walks by! But that's no elephant—it's Molang in a costume! Molang is trying to figure out what to wear to the Halloween party. Should Molang be an elephant? Or maybe a wizard?

Piu Piu has the best idea yet. Molang should be a mummy!

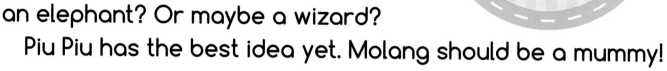

The doorbell rings and Piu Piu opens the door to find Molang wrapped up from ear to toe. Piu Piu grabs the finished jack-o'-lantern and asks Molang to put it on top of the scarecrow.

"Hey, Piu Piu!" Molang says, walking down the stairs. Piu Piu is confused. If Molang is here, who was the mummy at the door?

The two friends peek out the window and watch the mystery mummy walk away. Oh no! The pumpkin!

Molang and Piu Piu race down the road. When they reach the Halloween party, it is filled with vampires, wizards, and . . . lots and LOTS of mummies!

But there, in the crowd, they spy something orange. They start to walk down the hill, but Molang trips on the costume's mummy wrappings and sends Piu Piu tumbling, too!

Piu Piu and the pumpkin roll through the party and tumble right onto a bench, where the mystery mummy is sitting. Molang lands on the bench hard, sending Piu Piu and the pumpkin into the air.

The pumpkin is getting away!
Molang and Piu Piu chase it up and down the hills.
They chase it through the trees, swinging along on
the mummy's wrappings.

One of their friends rides by and Molang has an idea. They borrow their friend's scooter and take off after the runaway pumpkin once again.

The pumpkin bounces back through the trees and crashes the party.

Everyone is down—literally!

Molang and Piu Piu apologize for their pumpkin. To make it up to their friends, they decide to invite everyone over to their house.

Molang and Piu Piu finally finish the scarecrow. Now the party can really get started!

After the party, their friends start to go home, but two of them stay. They brought a spooky movie to top off their spooky day.

They watch as a monster sneaks into a house.
This movie is sort of scary.

Then the monster hides under a bed and waits. This movie is really scary!

By the end of the movie, everyone is frightened. They turn on the lights. What a relief! But Piu Piu is still afraid!

A little nervous, their friends pack up their movie and head home . . .

But Piu Piu can't shake the jitters. And when Piu Piu walks into the bedroom, it seems very dark. What if that monster is under the bed?

Molang checks under Piu Piu's bed. There is nothing there!

But Piu Piu is still nervous.

Molang comes up with a plan to tie string and bells all around Piu Piu's bed. This way, if a monster comes to get them, they will hear the bells and wake up!

Molang says good night again and Piu Piu heads back to bed . . .

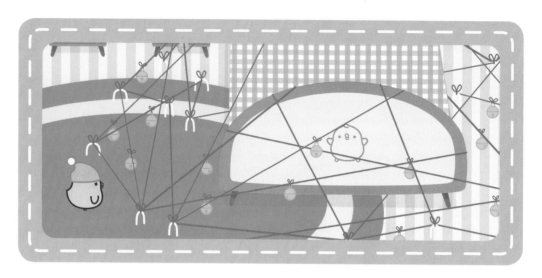

Except, how will Piu Piu get past all that string?
Piu Piu jumps, ducks, and dives . . .
And misses the bed. Piu Piu is caught in their trap!

Molang comes to the rescue and quickly untangles Piu Piu. But Piu Piu is still nervous.

Piu Piu's best friend has one last idea. Molang goes to the edge of the room and takes a running leap.

Molang lands on Piu Piu's bed with a giant *thump*. The bed legs wobble and break. *Thunk* goes the bed. Now no monsters can hide under it!

Piu Piu cheers. Today was filled with spooky, scary fun, but now the two friends can go to sleep, safe and sound.